James Mayhew

*For my sister Kate
who first introduced me to the
"Dolly Music"*

Many thanks to Antonio Reche-Martinez
for being the perfect toymaker.

ORCHARD BOOKS
First published in Great Britain in 2017 by The Watts Publishing Group
This edition first published in 2018

1 3 5 7 9 10 8 6 4 2

Text and illustrations © James Mayhew, 2017

A CIP catalogue record for this book is available from the British Library.

ISBN 978 1 40833 686 1
Printed and bound in China

Orchard Books
An imprint of Hachette Children's Group
Part of The Watts Publishing Group Limited
Carmelite House
50 Victoria Embankment
London EC4Y 0DZ

An Hachette UK Company
www.hachette.co.uk
www.hachettechildrens.co.uk

James Mayhew
presents

Ella Bella
BALLERINA
~ and ~
The Magic Toyshop

ORCHARD

Ella Bella danced along the street to her ballet class. Her teacher, Madame Rosa, was waiting by the door of the old theatre.
"Come inside darling!" she said.

All the other children were chattering excitedly on the stage. Madame Rosa had put out her magical musical box, surrounded by toys and dolls.

 "Please may we play with them?" asked Ella Bella.

 "Why not *dance* with them!" said Madame Rosa, as she opened the musical box.

"Oh, what funny music!" laughed the children.
"I call it Dolly Music," said Madame Rosa. "It comes from the ballet *La Boutique Fantasque*. The story takes place in a toyshop full of dancing dolls, all looked after by the kind toymaker."

"I'd *love* a dancing doll," sighed Ella Bella. "Would you love and look after it?" asked Madame Rosa. "Oh yes!" said Ella Bella. "I would!"

After the ballet lesson, Ella Bella stayed behind to tidy up. She saw the lid of the musical box was open and couldn't resist starting the music again.

As she danced around with one of the dolls, she noticed a door to a shop. A toyshop.

"Our first customer of the day," welcomed the kindly toymaker and his apprentice.

"Oh, what a lot of dolls!" gasped Ella Bella, gazing at all their colourful faces and costumes. They looked almost real.

Just then, in bustled two families
demanding to see the finest dolls.
"Which one first?" wondered the toymaker.
"I have so many boxes and so many dolls . . ."
He wound up a pair of Italian dolls with china
faces. And they began to dance.

Next, the toymaker opened
a box and out danced some
playing cards.

Ella Bella opened
another box and found two
toy poodle dogs who twirled
delicately on their paws.

Just when everyone thought
there could be nothing better,
the toymaker revealed his
Russian dolls.

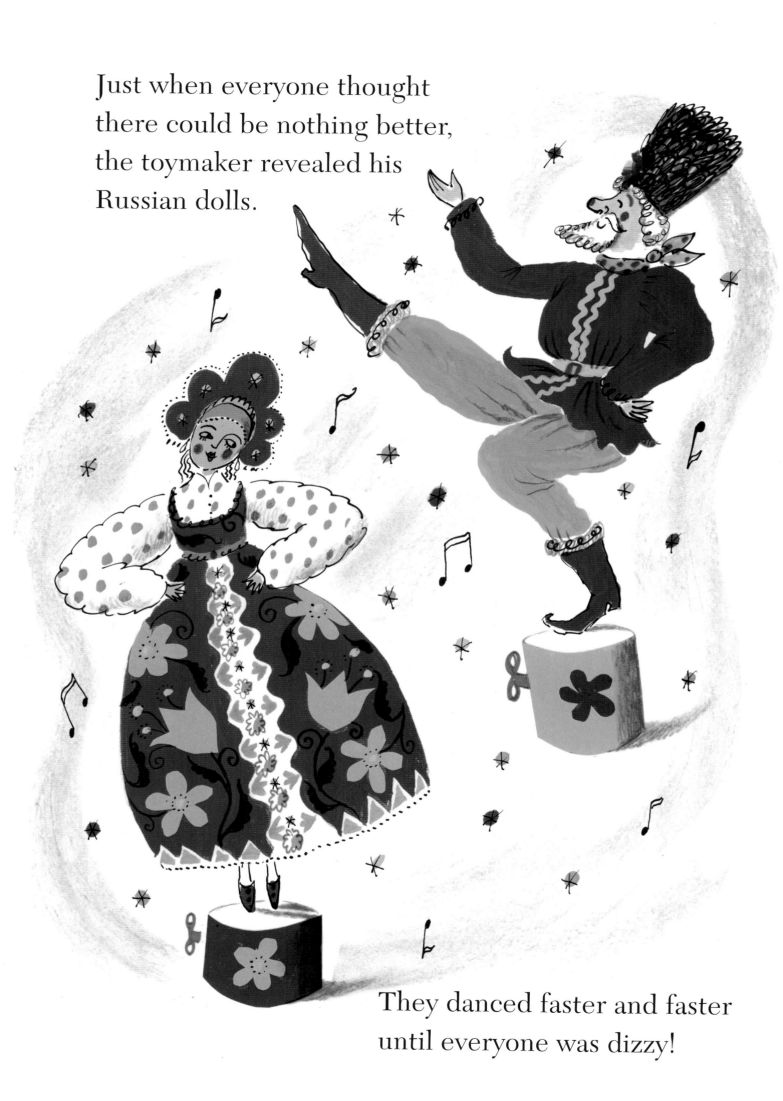

They danced faster and faster
until everyone was dizzy!

Neither family could decide which dolls to buy.
The toymaker smiled. "In this box," he said,
"I have the most beautiful, the most fabulous
dolls of all."

He opened the lid. Everyone held their breath . . .

There was a pair of dazzling dolls dressed as can-can dancers! They had the most colourful frills and ribbons.

When they danced it was hard to believe they were only dolls.

"We'll buy them!"
said one family.
"No, we want them!"
said the other family.
They argued and argued
and got very cross.

Ella Bella thought they didn't
deserve such lovely dolls.

"Oh dear," said the toymaker. "Really they belong together, but . . . I suppose I could sell you one each?"

After some more arguing the families agreed and promised to collect the dolls the next day.

By now it was late. The toymaker closed
the shop and everyone went home.

Everyone except Ella Bella. She was
worried about the can-can dolls.
How sad they looked, sitting together
by the window.

But then, as the moon rose in the sky, they
slowly began to dance all by themselves . . .

Ella Bella gasped. "Oh, this really is a *magic* toyshop!" she said.

All the other dolls came to life. "Please can you help the can-can dancers?" they asked Ella Bella.

"They are very much in love. It would break their hearts to be parted."

"There are so many boxes," said Ella Bella.
"Perhaps they can hide!"

"Oh, yes!" said the can-can dancers. So Ella Bella
and all the dolls danced around the shop with the
boxes until the can-can dolls were safely hidden.

Soon it was morning and in came
the toymaker and his apprentice.
Next came the two families.
"We want our dolls!" they demanded.
The toymaker began searching through
his shop, opening this box and that.
"I am sure they are here somewhere . . ."

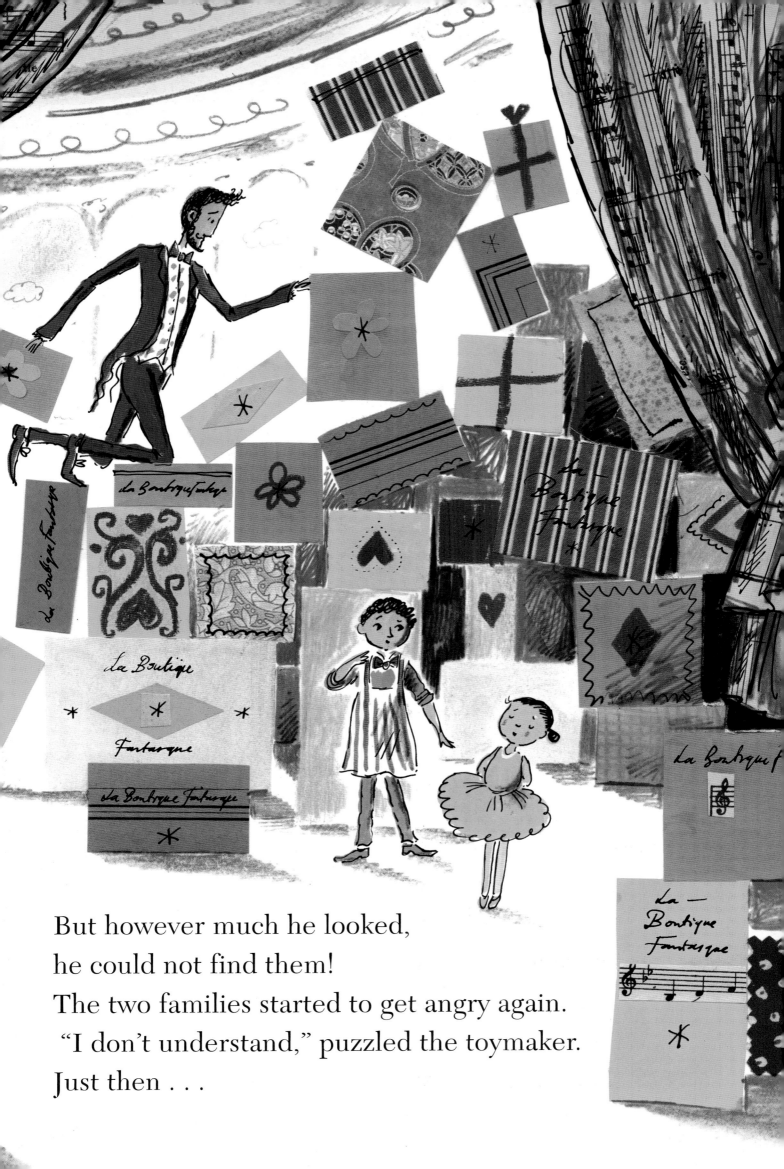

But however much he looked,
he could not find them!
The two families started to get angry again.
"I don't understand," puzzled the toymaker.
Just then . . .

. . . all the dolls burst out of the boxes! They knew the toymaker was in trouble . . .

They danced and clapped and chased both families right out of the shop!

The toymaker began
to laugh. The apprentice
began to laugh. And Ella Bella
laughed too.

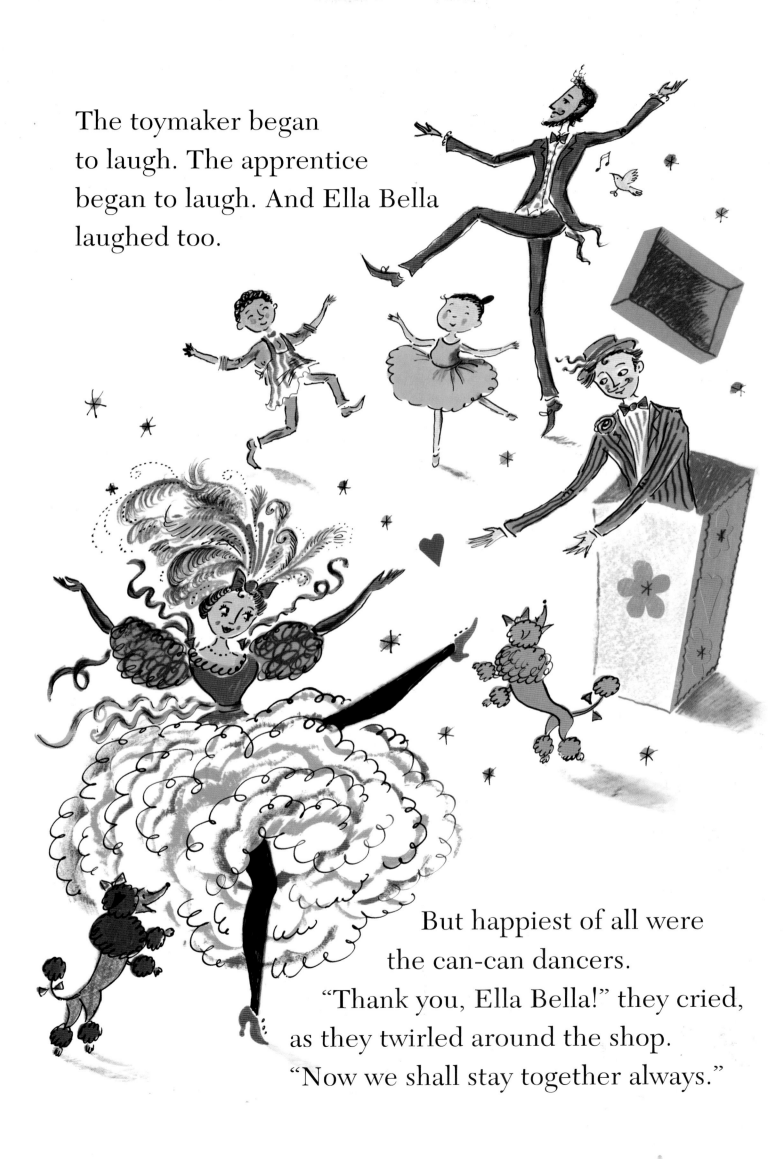

But happiest of all were
the can-can dancers.
"Thank you, Ella Bella!" they cried,
as they twirled around the shop.
"Now we shall stay together always."

The toymaker and his apprentice decided to take the rest of the day off. As Ella Bella danced through the door, the music stopped and she found herself back on the stage.

She gathered up the toys and took them to
Madame Rosa.
"Thank you, darling," she said. "Would you
like to take a doll home with you?"

"Oh no, thank you," said Ella Bella. "I think they
will be much happier if they all stay together."

On her way home Ella Bella thought about her own dolls. She couldn't wait to tell them about her adventure. "Who knows," she thought, "one of them might be magic too!"

La Boutique Fantasque

There are lots of ballets with dancing toys, like Coppelia and The Nutcracker. But The Magic Toyshop is, perhaps, the most charming of all.

The proper name for this ballet is *La Boutique Fantasque*, and it was first performed in London by the Ballet Russe company, in 1919. The story is set on the French Riviera, in the late 19th century. The scenery was painted by a famous French artist called André Derain.

The music was written by two composers, both from Italy. Gioachino Rossini wrote lots of famous music, including an opera about Cinderella called *La Cenerentola*. His music is full of sunshine and laughter. After Rossini died, Ottorino Respighi found some piano music by him and thought it would make a lovely ballet. So, he arranged it for a big orchestra, and this made the music very famous. There are all sorts of wonderful tunes, from the Italian Tarantella (a traditional dance inspired by the tarantula spider!), to a dazzling Russian dance and, of course, the French can-can.

Today the ballet is often performed by dance schools, as it has just one act, and so gives young dancers the perfect opportunity to dance in a full production, and share this enchanting music and magical story with their audience.